SUPER
STANLEY
AND THE
NEW BABY

by Sara Lewis

Published by Kingdom First Books
kingdomfirstbooks@gmail.com

ISBN 978-1-8384235-0-6

SUPER
STANLEY
AND THE
NEW BABY

by Sara Lewis

This book belongs to

. . . .

for Stanley
and Jake

Since Mummy brought
New Baby home,
Stanley sometimes feels alone.

Mummy's always having to
feed the baby, clean his poo,

change his nappy when he wees,
and now she doesn't play with me.

I want to send
New Baby back

up to the moon
on a jet pack!

Or send him away
on a plane,

and then life will be
good again.

But Mummy said,
"No way, no way!
Those ideas are not OK

because he is your
little brother,
and you need to love
each other."

So from now on,
I want to be
the best big brother
I can be.

I want to be a SUPER BRO
to help my brother
learn and grow.

I'll do a dance to
make him giggle,

teach him how to
wave and wiggle...

and when he gets a little bigger,
we can play with
trucks and diggers!

So I'm happy in the end
because I have a new
best friend,

and I can love my family,
especially the new baby.

the end

Also available!
Perfect for new big sisters.

SUPER
SUZIE
AND THE
NEW BABY

by Sara Lewis

ISBN 978-1-8384235-1-3

Printed in Great Britain
by Amazon